PYRAMID OF THE SUN
PYRAMID OF THE MOON

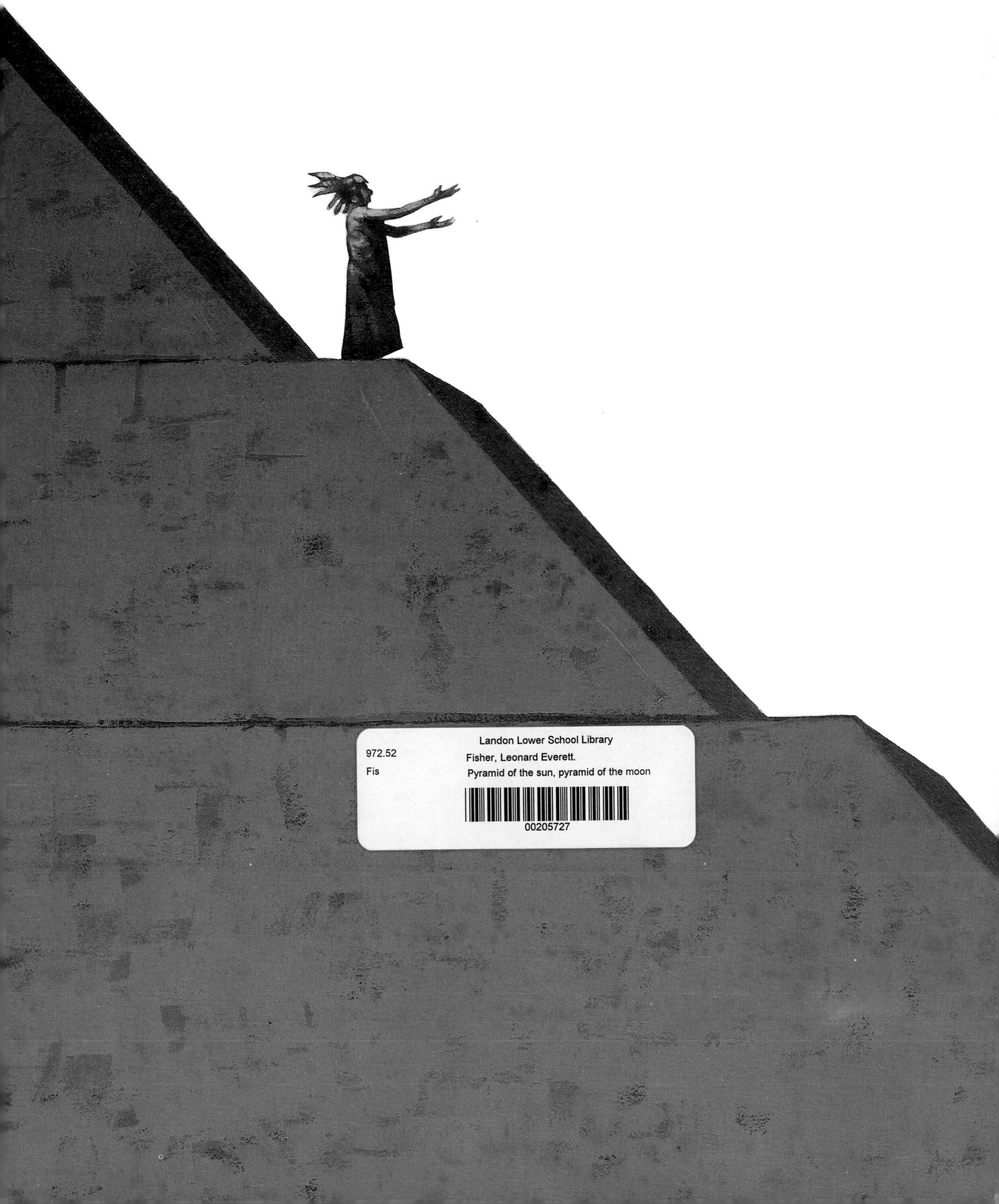

PYRAMID OF THE SUN
PYRAMID OF THE MOON

LEONARD EVERETT FISHER

MACMILLAN PUBLISHING COMPANY

NEW YORK

VALLEY OF MEXICO HISTORY, circa 150 B.C. – 1521

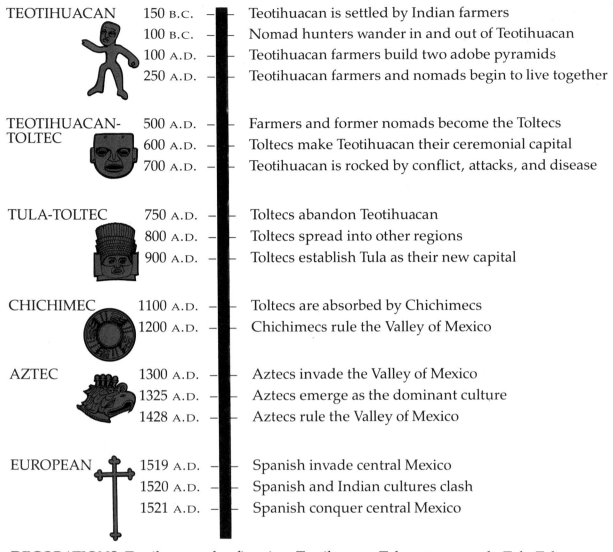

TEOTIHUACAN	150 B.C.	Teotihuacan is settled by Indian farmers
	100 B.C.	Nomad hunters wander in and out of Teotihuacan
	100 A.D.	Teotihuacan farmers build two adobe pyramids
	250 A.D.	Teotihuacan farmers and nomads begin to live together
TEOTIHUACAN-TOLTEC	500 A.D.	Farmers and former nomads become the Toltecs
	600 A.D.	Toltecs make Teotihuacan their ceremonial capital
	700 A.D.	Teotihuacan is rocked by conflict, attacks, and disease
TULA-TOLTEC	750 A.D.	Toltecs abandon Teotihuacan
	800 A.D.	Toltecs spread into other regions
	900 A.D.	Toltecs establish Tula as their new capital
CHICHIMEC	1100 A.D.	Toltecs are absorbed by Chichimecs
	1200 A.D.	Chichimecs rule the Valley of Mexico
AZTEC	1300 A.D.	Aztecs invade the Valley of Mexico
	1325 A.D.	Aztecs emerge as the dominant culture
	1428 A.D.	Aztecs rule the Valley of Mexico
EUROPEAN	1519 A.D.	Spanish invade central Mexico
	1520 A.D.	Spanish and Indian cultures clash
	1521 A.D.	Spanish conquer central Mexico

DECORATIONS: Teotihuacan clay figurine, Teotihuacan-Toltec stone mask, Tula-Toltec stone warrior head, Chichimec pottery dish, Aztec gold eagle head, Spanish Christian cross

With appreciation to Dr. Richard E. Blanton, Professor of Anthropology, Purdue University

Library of Congress Cataloging-in-Publication Data
Fisher, Leonard Everett.
Pyramid of the sun, pyramid of the moon/Leonard Everett Fisher. —1st ed.   p.   cm.
Summary: Discusses the history of the pyramids of Teotihuacan and of the Aztecs, how they evolved from the Toltecs, how they lived and worshipped, and how they were overcome by the Spaniards.
ISBN 0-02-735300-1
1. Aztecs—Social life and customs—Juvenile literature. 2. Toltecs—Social life and customs—Juvenile literature. 3. Indians of Mexico—San Juan Teotihuacan—Social life and customs—Juvenile literature. 4. Teotihuacan Site (San Juan Teotihuacan, Mexico)—Juvenile literature. [1. Aztecs—Social life and customs. 2. Toltecs—Social life and customs. 3. Indians of Mexico—Social life and customs. 4. Teotihuacan Site (San Juan Teotihuacan, Mexico)] I. Title.
F1219.76.S64F57 1988 972'.52—dc19
88-1410 CIP AC

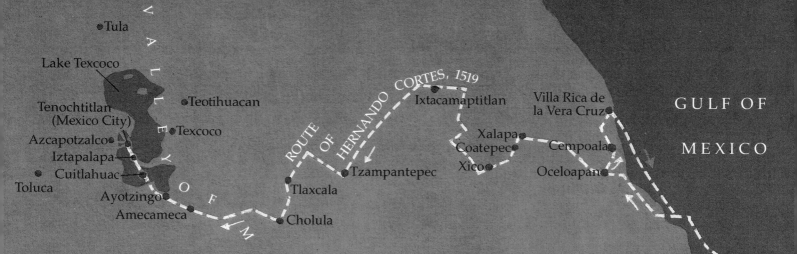

Tula

Lake Texcoco

•Teotihuacan

Tenochtitlan
(Mexico City)

•Texcoco

Azcapotzalco

Iztapalapa

Cuitlahuac

Toluca

Ayotzingo

Amecameca

V A L L E Y   O F   M E X I C O

ROUTE OF HERNANDO CORTES, 1519

Ixtacamaptitlan

Villa Rica de
la Vera Cruz

GULF OF
MEXICO

Xalapa
Coatepec

Cempoala

Xico

Oceloapan

Tzampantepec

Tlaxcala

Cholula

MEXICO

PACIFIC

OCEAN

THE VALLEY OF MEXICO, 1519

miles 0   25   50   75   100

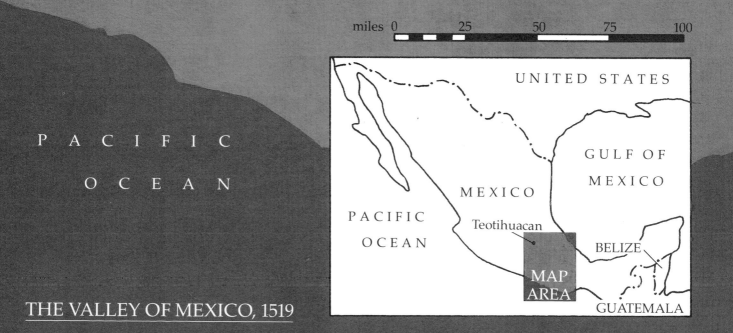

UNITED STATES

GULF OF
MEXICO

MEXICO

PACIFIC
OCEAN

Teotihuacan

BELIZE

MAP
AREA

GUATEMALA

There is a spot in the Valley of Mexico that the Aztecs called Teotihuacan, the "place of the gods." The Indians who settled there about 150 B.C., many centuries before the Aztecs arrived, were farmers. After some two hundred fifty years, they built two great pyramids of adobe, or sun-dried clay bricks, from which they watched the sun and moon rise and set. Later, the Aztecs named these structures Pyramid of the Sun and Pyramid of the Moon.

Wandering tribes of hunters who worshipped serpents and jaguars settled among the valley dwellers. Little by little they adopted the farmers' ideas, added their own, and formed a new culture. Soon they were all known as Toltecs, or "those who are civilized."

The Toltecs grew cotton, corn, beans, and peppers. They were weavers, carpenters, potters, and stonecarvers who made dark, glassy knives. More important, the Toltecs were master builders eager to develop Teotihuacan into a religious center where they would worship the sun, the moon, serpents, and jaguars.

The Toltecs turned dusty eight-square-mile Teotihuacan into a city of cement streets and avenues, stately houses, and magnificent temples. Never had there been a place like it in central Mexico—or anywhere else in the Western Hemisphere!

Towering over Teotihuacan were its mighty Pyramid of the Sun and Pyramid of the Moon. The pyramids were filled solid with rubble, faced with stone, and plastered over to make their surfaces smooth. Steps running up the front of each pyramid led to temples at the top.

The Toltecs had transformed Teotihuacan into a holy city and a craft and trade center of two hundred thousand people. Ordinary Toltecs were forbidden to live near the pyramids and temples. Only priests, nobles, and the slaves of both could remain there. Everyone else lived in special districts or in other Toltec towns—Tula, Toluca, Cholula, and Azcapotzalco.

Looming over the flat landscape was the Pyramid of the Sun, the larger of the two pyramids. It was a series of platforms soaring more than two hundred feet skyward from a square base seven hundred and forty feet on each side. From its heights, Toltec priests saw the sun rise and set every day. It seemed to them that the sun rose from the earth and returned to the earth. They believed that this was the daily birth, death, and rebirth of the sun god, ruler of the sky. And they believed that the earth goddess was his mother. Steps at the base of the pyramid led to rooms beneath it. No one knows the use of these dark places.

The Pyramid of the Sun stood beside a broad, mile-long avenue lined with small temples and palaces. The avenue was called the Avenue of the Dead by the Aztecs. They believed that Toltec kings who had died and become gods were buried along its route.

At the north end of the Avenue of the Dead stood the smaller Pyramid of the Moon. From its several levels Toltec priests watched the moon rise and set every night, just as they had watched the sun earlier. And, like the sun's comings and goings, the priests viewed the moon's as a process of constant birth, death, and rebirth—of the moon goddess, wife of the sun god, ruler of the night sky.

Toltec priests carefully measured the travels of the sun and the moon across the sky. They created two calendars. One was a three-hundred-sixty-five-day calendar that kept track of the farming seasons. The other, a two-hundred-sixty-day calendar, kept track of religious ceremonies. After fifty-two years, these no longer worked, and the Toltecs made new calendars.

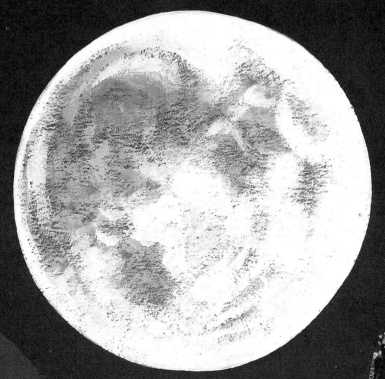

At the southern end of the Avenue of the Dead was a small plat-
form on which sat the Temple of Quetzalcoatl, the "feathered
serpent," god of learning. The Toltecs believed Quetzalcoatl had
brought them civilization, had taught them how to grow food,
weave, carve, cut stone, and build a city. They feared
that if they did not use the knowledge Quetzalcoatl had given
them, the great god would return to his kingdom in the east.

Besides the sun and the moon, serpents and jaguars, the Toltecs also worshipped the stars, rain, plants, and wind. On religious holidays and special occasions great crowds gathered to watch the priests conduct ceremonies on the pyramids and in the temples of Teotihuacan.

Between 700 and 750, famine, disease, revolts, and attacks from uncivilized tribes put an end to the sacred city of Teotihuacan. Those who survived fled south and west, leaving Teotihuacan a vast, empty, silent ruin. And, according to fleeing Toltec priests, Quetzalcoatl returned to the east as he had threatened. Still the Toltecs continued to forge an empire in central Mexico from their new capital, Tula. But by 1100, the Toltecs no longer dominated the region. Wandering tribes called Chichimecs ruled the valley.

With the Toltecs gone from Teotihuacan, the Chichimecs came often to the deserted city to bury their dead. To them, as well, Teotihuacan was sacred ground.

When warring tribes bent on the conquest of central Mexico migrated to the valley, the Chichimecs disappeared. These conquerors were the Aztecs, sometimes called Mexicas.

By the time the Aztecs controlled central Mexico—about 1428—Teotihuacan had stood in silence for around seven hundred years. The mystery and power of the city where the wind made the only sound struck the Aztecs as it had the Chichimecs. They, too, were certain that the gods had not left Teotihuacan.

The Aztecs viewed the Toltecs as their ancestors. They believed the ancient gods and goddesses continued to rule the universe. They held sacred every pebble and blade of grass in ghostly Teotihuacan.

The Aztecs raised their own soaring pyramids. The tallest was the Great Temple Pyramid in Tenochtitlan, the Aztec capital. Tenochtitlan was built on a lake. Some of its streets were canals, and long causeways connected it to the lakeshore. The Great Temple Pyramid loomed over the watery city where nearly a quarter of a million Aztecs lived and planned fearful ceremonies.

To keep the gods happy, the Aztecs took enemy warriors alive and tore their beating hearts from their chests on the stone altar of the Great Temple Pyramid. For rituals like the New Fire Ceremony, which marked the end of one fifty-two-year calendar cycle and the beginning of another, they required a special person and place for sacrifice. Aztec priests occasionally took a royal captive to Teotihuacan. After feasting the prisoner, they dragged him up to the altar of the Pyramid of the Sun. There, with the quick slash of a glassy knife, they cut his heart from him and burned it to feed the sun god on his journey across the sky. Then, to symbolize new life, they lit the sun god's flame in his open chest. Similar ceremonies took place on the Pyramid of the Moon, where human victims also were sacrificed to the gods.

Montezuma II, the powerful Aztec emperor who ruled from 1503 to 1520, often traveled to Teotihuacan, where he climbed the steps of the pyramids and asked the gods to show him the future. One day the priests told him that soon Quetzalcoatl would return from the east to reclaim his land.

Later, when Montezuma heard that an army of iron-clad beings on strange four-legged beasts was nearing Tenochtitlan from the east, he believed the leader to be Quetzalcoatl. He, Montezuma, would give the god whatever he wanted! He sent gifts to the oncoming army and rushed to the pyramids to seek guidance and long life. Messengers followed him there with the news that the approaching army was not an army of gods led by Quetzalcoatl, but an army of men led by a man like himself.

The iron-clad men were Spanish soldiers. Their strange beasts were horses! They had come to the land of the Aztecs to claim it for themselves. Led by Hernando Cortes, whom Montezuma had believed to be Quetzalcoatl, they destroyed everything that stood in their way. Montezuma listened to reports of how Cortes and his men had ravaged other cities. Aztec knives and clubs were no match for the new, more terrible weapons that made loud noises. Montezuma was alarmed.

When Cortes reached the outskirts of Tenochtitlan, he saw a sight no white man had ever viewed. Before him was a neatly ordered city spread out on a shimmering lake, and larger than any city in Spain. This was what the Spaniards had come so far to have—the dazzling Aztec capital with its floating gardens, marketplaces, and gold.

On November 8, 1519, Montezuma, uncertain what Cortes wanted or might do, left his palace with nobles and warriors. He met Cortes and his army on one of the causeways. Against the advice of his priests, he invited Cortes to enter Tenochtitlan. The wary emperor hoped that if he provided Cortes and his men with a palace and showered them with gold and gifts, they would soon depart happily.

Montezuma showed off his city to Cortes and took Cortes to the home of his Toltec ancestors. In the shadows of the Pyramid of the Sun and the Pyramid of the Moon, he described his proud past.

Not long after, Montezuma was betrayed. Cortes made him a prisoner. Spanish soldiers murdered the Aztecs at a festival and stole their gold. In the months that followed, the Aztecs rioted over the Spanish treachery. Montezuma, in chains, tried to calm his angry people. But they blamed him for their troubles and attacked him. Montezuma died under a hail of arrows and stones.

Meanwhile, the Aztecs nearly defeated Cortes and his soldiers. The Spaniards escaped—but they would return. Thirty miles to the northeast, the Pyramid of the Sun and the Pyramid of the Moon stood in silent witness to the beginning of the end of the Aztec world.

MORE ABOUT THE PYRAMID OF THE SUN
AND THE PYRAMID OF THE MOON

Following Montezuma's death, two other Aztec kings tried to stop the growing Spanish power in central Mexico. Cuitlahuac, Montezuma's brother, was the first to succeed him. He became sick and died after a reign of four months. Montezuma's nephew, Cuauhtemoc, resisted another six months, then failed. He was captured in April 1521, tortured, and later hanged. Tenochtitlan fell into Spanish hands on August 13, 1521.

During this awful time, Tenochtitlan, the sparkling Aztec capital in the center of a shimmering lake, was destroyed. So complete was its devastation that both the Spaniards and the Aztecs left it to crumble and die. Today most of its rubble lies buried under Mexico City. Only the Pyramid of the Sun and the Pyramid of the Moon at Teotihuacan, "the place of the gods," remain. They are the oldest link between the Aztecs, the Toltecs, and the people of the Valley of Mexico.

A PRONUNCIATION GUIDE

Azcapotzalco	*Az-kah-pot-zal-koh*	Quetzalcoatl	*Kayt-zal-koh-atl*
Chichimec	*Chee-chee-mek*	Tenochtitlan	*Tay-notch-teet-lan*
Cholula	*Choh-loo-lah*	Teotihuacan	*Tay-oh-tee-wah-kan*
Cuitlahuac	*Kwee-tla-who-ak*	Toluca	*Toh-loo-kah*
Cuauhtemoc	*Kwow-tay-mok*	Tula	*Too-lah*
Mexica	*May-shee-kah*		